Something's Missing

Written by Meredith Costain

Illustrated by Martin Bailey

sundance™

sundance™

Published by
Sundance Publishing
33 Boston Post Road West
Suite 440
Marlborough, MA 01752
800-343-8204
www.sundancepub.com

Copyright © text Meredith Costain
Copyright © illustrations Martin Bailey

First published 2002 by
Pearson Education Australia Pty. Limited
95 Coventry Street
South Melbourne 3205 Australia
Exclusive United States Distribution: Sundance Publishing

Guided Reading Level K
Guided reading levels assigned by Sundance Publishing using the text
characteristics dscribed by Fountas & Pinnell in their book *Guided Reading,*
published by Heinemann.

ISBN 978-0-7608-6708-2

Printed in China

08/09-225495

Contents

Characters

Patrick tends to jump to conclusions.

Kim is good at solving mysteries.

Jason is a great soccer player.

Tammy believes in being fair.

Chapter One

Patrick's New Game

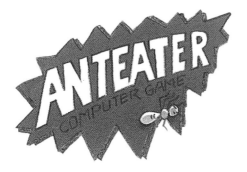

Patrick raced off the school bus and ran over to a group of kids playing baseball on the playground.

"Hi, Tim," he called. "Can I play?"

"Sure, if you want," replied Tim, keeping his eyes on the ball.

Patrick placed his backpack carefully next to the pile of bags at the edge of the field. Then he joined the game.

After the game, Patrick spotted Millie. He walked over to talk to her.

"I brought *Anteater*, my new computer game," he said, proudly patting the side of his backpack. "This is the best game ever. It has a lot more levels than other games."

"I bet it doesn't have graphics as good as *Nightmare II*," said Millie.

"Yes, it does," boasted Patrick. "Ten times better. And it's harder, too."

"Nothing's harder than *Nightmare II*," insisted Millie. "My sister's never gone past level three on that, and she's the best player in the school."

"Tell her to come to Daniel Sorenson's house tonight then," said Patrick. "We're going to play *Anteater*. I bet she won't even get past level one!"

Millie rolled her eyes. Patrick always thought he knew everything. One day it would get him into big trouble.

Just then, the bell rang. Everyone picked up their backpacks from the pile and raced off to class.

Patrick hung up his backpack in its usual place, between Michael's and Suzie's. He couldn't wait until school was over so he could show Daniel his new game. And he planned to show it to the kids in his class at lunchtime.

Chapter Two

The News Spreads

Patrick ran into the classroom, eager to tell everyone about *Anteater*.

"Hey, Tammy," he called, tapping her on the arm. "I got up to level six on my new game last night!"

"That's good," said Tammy. Then she turned back to talk to her friend.

Patrick turned to Raymond. "I brought in my game, Ray. Want to see it?"

"Maybe later," replied Raymond.

They're just jealous, Patrick thought. He sat down at his desk and took out his math book.

At morning recess, Miss Gomez asked Patrick, Jason, and Kim to help unpack some new playground equipment. So Patrick didn't get a chance to show anyone his new game. Instead, he told Jason and Kim all about it—again.

"It's got this giant anteater, see, and it eats armies of ants," explained Patrick. "You have to save the ants before it chews them all up."

Kim unpacked a soccer ball and bounced it off her knee. "Sounds gross," she said. "I'd much rather play soccer than computer games."

Jason picked up a baseball bat and practiced swinging it. "Are you trying out for the soccer team at lunchtime, Kim?" he asked.

"You bet," said Kim. "Nothing could keep me away. How about you, Patrick?"

"Nah," said Patrick. "I've got better things to do."

"Like telling everyone about his boring old *Anteater* computer game," whispered Jason to Kim.

Chapter Three

A Bad Surprise

After recess, Miss Gomez told the class about the pyramids and mummies of ancient Egypt. When she started to explain how the Egyptians made mummies, Jason raised his hand.

"Is it true that the Egyptians pulled the mummies' brains out through their noses with a hook?" he asked.

"That's right," said Miss Gomez.

"Then they packed the brains into special jars. They had jars for all of the different organs. Stomach. Heart. Intestines," continued Miss Gomez.

"That's really gross," said Kim.

Tammy raised her hand.

"Do you have some interesting information about mummies, Tammy?" asked Miss Gomez.

"N-no," stammered Tammy. "I just need to go to the girls' room."

"That's okay," said Miss Gomez with a smile. "You may go now."

Next, Miss Gomez explained to the class how pyramids were made. She explained that the Egyptians used secret passages and trapdoors. They were built to stop tomb raiders from stealing the pharaohs' treasures.

Miss Gomez had just finished drawing a diagram of a pyramid on the board when there was a knock at the door.

"Come in, Sam," said Miss Gomez. "I hope you haven't come to try and steal our treasure!"

Everyone laughed.

Sam walked over to Miss Gomez and handed her a note. He tapped his swollen cheek. "I had to go to the dentist."

"That's all right, Sam," she replied. "Take your seat. Now, class, please open your books to page 56."

Soon it was lunchtime, and Patrick was the first person out the door.

Finally he'd be able to show everyone his new game. When the other kids saw the graphics on the front of the box, they'd know how good the game was. This was going to be fun!

Patrick stuck his hand inside his backpack and felt around. There was his lunch box. There was his drink bottle. But where was his computer game? Oh, no! he thought. His *Anteater* game was gone!

Chapter Four

Patrick Accuses

Someone had stolen his *Anteater* game! Patrick thought. "Miss Gomez!" he called. "Please come here, Miss Gomez!"

The teacher came running. "What is it, Patrick?" she asked. "Are you hurt?"

"No!" said Patrick. He held up his backpack. "Someone's stolen my new game! It's not here!"

Miss Gomez peered into the backpack.

"Are you sure?" she asked.

"Yes," Patrick replied quickly. "I put it in there myself this morning." His eyes narrowed. "Someone from this class took it, and I know who it was. It was Raymond."

Miss Gomez folded her arms. "And how do you know that, Patrick?"

"Because I told him I was bringing it to school today. Right, Raymond?"

Miss Gomez looked at Raymond. "Is this true, Raymond?" she asked.

"Sure," said Raymond. "But that doesn't mean I took it. I don't even like to play computer games."

"That's not true!" shouted Patrick. "I've seen you playing them!"

"Calm down, Patrick," Miss Gomez said. "Each of you please get your backpack."

"Mine is at home," Raymond said. "I forgot to bring it."

Everyone began talking at once. Could one of them really be a thief?

Kim looked at Jason. "I hope this doesn't make us late for soccer tryouts," she muttered.

"Does anyone have anything they'd like to say?" asked Miss Gomez, as they all sat down at their desks. "Perhaps someone took Patrick's game by accident? Now would be the time to let him know."

But no one put up their hand.

"I bet it was Tammy," said Patrick.

Tammy jumped up. "No way!" she cried. "That's not fair."

"Sit down, Tammy," said her teacher calmly. "Why do you think it was Tammy, Patrick?"

"Tammy left the class to go to the girls' room," said Patrick. "She could've taken it from my backpack on the way back, and put it in hers. Or she could have hidden it under her sweater. It's probably in her desk right now!"

Tammy jumped up from her chair. "I went to the girls' room. Then I came right back," she insisted. "You can look in my desk all you like," she told Patrick, "but you're never going to find it. And you can look in my backpack, too."

Tammy picked up her backpack and emptied its contents onto the floor. Out fell a lunch box, a drink bottle, a library book, a yo-yo, and two sticks of chewing gum. But there was no sign of an *Anteater* computer game.

"Thank you, Tammy," said Miss Gomez. "You may sit down now."

"Patrick, please apologize to Tammy," said Miss Gomez.

"Sorry," muttered Patrick. "But if it wasn't Tammy, then I bet it was Sam. He was late for class. He could have taken the game from my backpack on his way in," said Patrick, pointing at Sam.

"Now, Patrick, slow down! You can't just accuse everyone," said Miss Gomez.

"I didn't take your game, Patrick," said Sam. "Go ahead and look in my backpack." Sam unzipped it so Patrick and Miss Gomez could look inside. "But I did see something in the bushes near the main gate on my way in. What color was the box, Patrick?"

"Bright red," said Patrick excitedly, "with pictures of black ants all over it."

"Red," muttered Sam. "I think this box might have been red, too."

"Why didn't you pick it up?" asked Patrick.

"I was just about to when Mrs. Jackson walked by and told me to get to class," explained Sam. "Maybe it's still there. Should I check, Miss Gomez?"

"That would be very helpful," his teacher answered.

Kim looked out the window. The other kids were already streaming out of their classrooms. If they didn't find the thief soon, she and Jason would miss trying out for the soccer team.

Everyone was whispering about how unfair it was that they all had to wait for Patrick's game to be found. They all looked up hopefully when Sam came back holding a red cardboard box.

Chapter Five

The Mystery Is Solved

Sam placed the box on Miss Gomez's desk. "Sorry," he said. "It was only a candy box. Looks like your game is still missing, Patrick."

Jason put up his hand. "Please, Miss Gomez. Can we go out to lunch now? It's important."

"So is finding Patrick's game," Miss Gomez replied.

"Now, Patrick," she said patiently, "think carefully. Are you sure you put the game in your bag this morning? Perhaps you left it at home by mistake."

"I know I packed it, Miss Gomez. Just like I know someone in this class took it." Patrick pointed an accusing finger at two kids in the back of the room.

"Michael and Suzie," Patrick said. "Their backpacks are right next to mine in the hall. One of them could have easily slipped the game out of my backpack and put it into their own."

Michael's face flushed red. "Are you calling me a thief, Patrick?"

"If you want to look in my backpack, go ahead!" snapped Suzie. She sped across the room and dumped her backpack out on the desk in front of Patrick.

"Quiet!" called Miss Gomez, as everyone started talking at once.

By now Kim was getting desperate. If only she could do something. She loved reading mystery stories and watching detective shows on TV. Maybe there was a clue that would help to explain the computer game's disappearance.

Kim looked at the two blue backpacks
sitting on Patrick's desk. They were almost
identical, right down to the label on the
front pocket. Most of the other backpacks
looked the same, too. It gave her an idea.
She put up her hand. "Excuse me, Miss
Gomez. Maybe Patrick should check his
backpack again—in front of all of us."

Miss Gomez smiled. "Good idea, Kim.
Patrick, take another good look in your
backpack. Perhaps your game is hiding in
there somewhere."

Patrick put his hand inside his bag and pulled out a drink bottle. Then he pulled out a lunch box. His stomach rumbled. He sure was getting hungry. He could at least see what his mom had packed for today.

Patrick opened his lunch box and took out a sandwich. Tuna fish! Yuck! He hated tuna fish. His mother would never make him a tuna fish sandwich.

Patrick opened the drink bottle. There was orange juice in it. But he was allergic to oranges! What was going on?

Patrick poked around inside the bag and pulled out a library book. The book was about riding horses. He knew that he wasn't reading that book.

Patrick's face turned red. He looked up at Miss Gomez. "Umm . . . I don't think this is my bag," he mumbled.

Chapter Six

Patrick's Apology

It took only a few more minutes for the mystery to be solved. Patrick finally realized that he must have picked up the wrong backpack from the pile near the field that morning.

Patrick asked Miss Gomez if he could leave the room to find Millie and the other kids who had played baseball. He was sure that the backpack he had taken was Millie's.

Millie had gone straight to a music lesson and hadn't had lunch yet. So she hadn't realized there had been a mix-up.

Patrick brought his backpack into class with him. Red-faced, he held up the *Anteater* game so everyone could see it.

Several kids at the back of the room began to whisper angrily.

"Quiet, everyone," said Miss Gomez. "I think you owe the kids you accused an apology, Patrick. Don't you?"

"I'm sorry," said Patrick, looking straight ahead.

But nobody believed him. As soon as Miss Gomez dismissed them, everyone surrounded Patrick on the steps outside the classroom.

"Thanks for making me miss soccer tryouts," said Jason. "Now I won't be able to make the team."

"Me either," said Kim. "You're so selfish, Patrick. You never care about anyone else but yourself."

"And how could you accuse us of stealing? How would you like to be called a thief?" asked Tammy, moving in close to him.

"Yeah," said Michael and Suzie, moving even closer. "Not much fun, is it?"

"Thief, thief, thief!" shouted the rest of the kids.

"I . . . I'm . . ." Patrick stammered.

"You're what?" asked Tammy. "Sorry? Then let's hear you say it like you really mean it this time."

Patrick looked at the sea of accusing faces in front of him. They were right, he thought to himself. It wasn't fun to be accused of something.

It was much worse when you knew that
you didn't do anything wrong. Patrick hung
his head. "I'm really sorry for calling you a
thief, Tammy. And you, too, Raymond.
And Michael and Suzie and Sam. And I'm
really sorry I made you miss soccer tryouts,
Kim and Jason," Patrick said. "M-maybe I
could talk to the coach for you. Then I
could try to explain what happened and
why you were both too late."

"And explain about how you were wrong, too," insisted Kim.

Patrick nodded. It was going to be hard to tell another teacher how wrong he'd been. But he owed it to his classmates. Besides, computer games—even *Anteater*—wouldn't be much fun without friends to help you play them.